Disney
PRINCESS
Bedtime Stories

Disney PRESS

LOS ANGELES • NEW YORK

Contents

Sleeping Beauty
Aurora's Slumber Party 1

Tangled
Bedtime for Max 17

Beauty and the Beast
The Bedtime Story 33

The Princess and the Frog
Tiana's Long Night 51

Mulan
Mushu's Tale 67

Brave
A Merida and Mum Day 83

Pocahontas
Lost and Found 101

Cinderella
A Nighttime Stroll 119

The Little Mermaid
The Ghost Lights 137

Tangled
Rapunzel's Campout 153

The Princess and the Frog
The Best-Friend Sleepover 171

The Little Mermaid
Ariel's Night Lights 187

Sleeping Beauty
Briar Rose to the Rescue 205

Beauty and the Beast
Star Stories 223

Snow White and the Seven Dwarfs
Grumpy's Not Sleepy 239

Cinderella
Bedtime for Gus 257

Brave
The Princess and the Kelpie 271

Aladdin
Abu Monkeys Around 287

All illustrations by the Disney Storybook Art Team

Collection copyright © 2017 Disney Enterprises, Inc.

All rights reserved. Published by Disney Press, an imprint of Disney Book Group. No part of this book may be reproduced or transmitted in any form or by any means, electronic or mechanical, including photocopying, recording, or by any information storage and retrieval system, without written permission from the publisher. For information address Disney Press, 1101 Flower Street, Glendale, California 91201.

Printed in the United States of America

Second Edition, September 2017

10 9 8 7 6 5 4 3

Library of Congress Catalog Card Number: 2015955213

FAC-038091-19049

ISBN 978-1-4847-4711-7

For more Disney Press fun, visit www.disneybooks.com

SUSTAINABLE FORESTRY INITIATIVE Certified Sourcing
www.sfiprogram.org
SFI-00993
Logo Applies to Text Stock Only

Disney PRINCESS
Sleeping Beauty

Aurora's Slumber Party

PRINCESS AURORA LOVED BEING married to Prince Phillip and living in the castle. But she missed her fairy friends, Flora, Fauna, and Merryweather.

One day Phillip told her he had to visit another kingdom overnight. "Why don't you invite the three good fairies to keep you company while I'm gone?" he said to Aurora.

"That's a wonderful idea!" Aurora replied. "I'll send them invitations right away!"

Flora, Fauna, and Merryweather were excited when they got their invitations. But when they arrived at the castle, Aurora was wearing her pajamas.

"Surprise!" Aurora cried. "It's a slumber party! You'd better change into your pajamas, too."

The fairies quickly changed into their pajamas and then used their magic to fill the room with music. In no time at all, everyone was dancing. The party was off to a great start!

Aurora took each fairy by the hand and whirled her left and right. As she twirled Fauna, Aurora's nightgown suddenly turned a lovely shade of blue.

"Oh, no. That won't do at all," Flora said. She pointed her wand at Aurora and turned the nightgown pink.

"Not so fast!" cried Merryweather, turning it blue again.

Back and forth the nightgown went until, finally, it settled to its usual color.

Suddenly, Flora picked up a pillow and swung it at Merryweather. Merryweather ducked and grabbed a pillow of her own. Fauna and Aurora stopped dancing and watched the fairies' pillow fight. Then they looked at each other and grabbed their own pillows.

Soon the room was covered in feathers, and the friends were out of breath from laughing.

"All that fighting has made me hungry. Maybe we should go downstairs and make a snack," Merryweather suggested.

In the kitchen, Merryweather made herself a triple-decker berry sandwich. It looked so good the other fairies raced over to make their own.

Soon the kitchen was abuzz with activity, everyone making her own bedtime snack.

Flora picked up her sandwich. As she bit into it, a dollop of cream flew across the room, right onto Aurora's face!

"Oops," Flora said. "I'm sorry, Princess."

But Aurora wasn't upset. In fact, she was laughing. Slumber parties were all about having fun, and she was having a great time!

"Let's read a story," Aurora suggested when she and the fairies went back upstairs. She and her friends gathered around the bed, and Flora read to them. Soon the fairies began to grow sleepy. Flora set the book aside, and everyone went to sleep.

Everyone, that is, except Flora! She was still too excited from the night. She tossed and turned. She flipped and flopped. And then she accidentally bonked Merryweather on the head!

Merryweather woke up and rubbed her head. "Ouch!" she cried. "Why did you hit me?"

"I didn't mean to," said Flora. "It's just that I can't fall asleep!"

"Well, now I can't sleep, either," said Merryweather.

All of their chatter woke up Fauna, who suggested they try counting sheep to fall asleep.

Flora and Merryweather agreed that Fauna's suggestion was worth trying. They lay down again and began to count.

"One, two, three . . ." Flora counted. All of a sudden, her sheep turned blue!

"Twelve . . . thirteen . . . fourteen . . ." Merryweather counted her blue sheep. But just when she had almost fallen asleep, Merryweather's sheep changed from blue to pink.

"Blue!" she cried, and changed them back.

"Pink!" Flora said, and the sheep changed color again.

Soon the two fairies were sitting up having another argument. But this time they woke Fauna *and* Aurora.

Aurora asked what was wrong, and the fairies told her about the pink and blue sheep. "Maybe there's a better way to fall asleep," Aurora said. She sat up and began to sing a lullaby to the fairies.

As her sweet voice carried across the room, the good fairies closed their eyes. Soon they were all fast asleep—even Flora!

"Ah, that's better," Aurora said. And then, humming the lullaby softly to herself, she pulled up the covers and went back to sleep.

Disney
PRINCESS

Tangled

Bedtime for Max

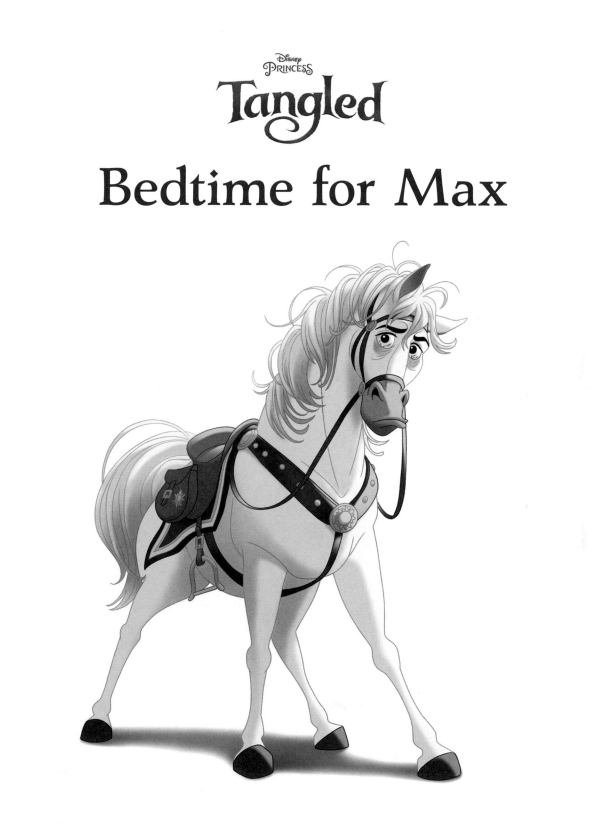

IT WAS A BEAUTIFUL morning in Corona. Everyone was enjoying the day. Everyone, that is, except the captain of the guard, Maximus. Max was hard at work, patrolling the streets for troublemakers and evildoers.

"Is it just me, or does Max look . . . strange?" Eugene asked Rapunzel as they strolled through town.

Rapunzel studied Max. He had dark circles under his eyes, and his normally neat mane was messy. "You're right," she said. "He looks like he hasn't slept in weeks!"

Eugene and Rapunzel found Max's second-in-command and asked him what was wrong with their friend.

"The captain has been so worried about doing a good job," the guard said, "that he hasn't been sleeping. No matter how many guards we put on duty, he insists that *he* needs to stay on patrol!"

Rapunzel was worried. Refusing to sleep *couldn't* be good for Max. "You know what this means," she told Eugene with a knowing look.

"Plan time?" Eugene asked.

"Plan time," Rapunzel agreed.

The two went off to figure out their plan. When they returned, they found Max running drills with his guards.

"Max!" Rapunzel cried. "I can't find Pascal anywhere! Can you help me find him? I'm afraid something might have happened!"

Max puffed out his chest. He was on the case! He started to sniff the ground, searching for the chameleon's scent.

Eugene and Rapunzel followed Max all around town. But Pascal was nowhere to be found.

Finally, as they turned toward the stables, Max caught the chameleon's scent.

The friends burst through the stable doors, eager to rescue Pascal. But he was fast asleep on a pile of hay!

"You found him! Great job, Max!" Rapunzel said.

"Say, Max, ol' buddy," Eugene said. "Since we're here, in the stables, with this nice pile of hay, what do you say to a nap?"

But Max just shook his head. He was too busy to take a break!

Rapunzel and Eugene looked at each other, disappointed. They had hoped that by tricking Max into following them to the stables, they could convince him to rest. But it looked like they were going to need another plan. Luckily, Eugene was on the case!

A little while later, Eugene and Rapunzel found Max inspecting ships that had just arrived at the harbor.

"Max! All the apples have been stolen from the orchard!" Eugene shouted.

Max knew he had to do something. He couldn't let a thief get away on his watch! He raced toward the apple orchard, his friends close behind.

Together, the team searched the orchard for clues about the missing apples. Soon Max spotted some footprints. He and his friends followed them back to the palace and into the kitchen . . . where they found a piping hot apple pie!

The apples hadn't been stolen after all. The chef had used them to make a special treat for the royal family's dinner.

"Apple pie! I love apple pie," Eugene exclaimed. "But it always makes me sleepy. Do you want a bite, Max?"

But Max just shook his head again. He didn't have time for pie! With the case of the missing apples solved, he had to get back to work. Corona needed him!

Disappointed, Eugene looked at Rapunzel. He had been sure that his plan was going to work!

"Maybe we can tire him out enough that he has to sleep?" Rapunzel suggested. "We just need to make him run around for a while." Suddenly, she had an idea.

"We have to get to the Snuggly Duckling!" Rapunzel told Max. "The pub thugs are in trouble!"

Trouble was the only word Max needed to hear. He motioned for Rapunzel and Eugene to hop on his back, and the three galloped toward the Snuggly Duckling.

Max burst into the Snuggly Ducking. He scanned the tavern, looking for the troublemakers. But everyone was gathered around the piano, singing and laughing.

Max looked at Rapunzel and Eugene, confused. No one was in trouble! With a sigh, he turned to leave.

"Wait, Max," Rapunzel said. "We're sorry we lied to you. We were just worried. The truth is we've been trying all day to make you rest."

"We were just trying to help," Eugene added.

"You *do* need a break, Max," Rapunzel said. "Can't you just stay for one song?"

Max was touched that his friends cared enough to spend the day trying to help him. With a whinny, he agreed. One song couldn't hurt.

Rapunzel grinned and whispered something in Hook Hand's ear. He nodded and then began to play a quiet, peaceful lullaby on the piano.

As Rapunzel sang along, she noticed Max swaying to the music. Slowly, his eyes began to close. Soon Max was fast asleep.

Eugene put a blanket over Max, and Rapunzel motioned for everyone to quickly leave the Snuggly Duckling. As the thugs quietly closed the door behind them, Rapunzel gave Eugene a hug. It had taken them all day, but they had finally gotten Max to take a well-deserved break!

Beauty and the Beast

The Bedtime Story

THE SUN WAS SETTING over the Beast's castle. Outside, the world was snowy and cold. But inside, Belle felt quite cozy. Though she wouldn't have believed it possible when she'd first arrived, Belle was enjoying her time there. She had spent the last few days outside, taking her horse, Philippe, on strolls and even having snowball fights with the Beast.

Somehow, against all odds, Belle was coming to think of the castle as home.

Belle watched through her window as the Beast walked Philippe to the stables. Pausing, he gave the horse an awkward—but kind— pat with his large paw. *There is more to him than meets the eye,* Belle thought.

Suddenly, Chip bounced in. "Belle! Belle! " he called. "It's story time!"

"Now, now, Chip," Mrs. Potts said, coming in behind her son. "You must wait for Belle to offer to read you a story. Perhaps she is tired and wishes to go to bed."

"I'm all right," Belle replied, smiling. She'd gotten into the habit of reading bedtime stories with her new friends, and she'd been looking forward to it all day. "Let's go down to the library."

"Yippee!" Chip cried as he bounced out of the room.

Lumiere and Cogsworth were already in the library when the trio arrived. The pair had pulled Belle's favorite chair close to the crackling fire. A warm blanket rested over the back, and a thick book with a worn leather cover sat on the seat.

"I thought perhaps we could read this one tonight," Cogsworth suggested, pointing at the book.

Lumiere peered at the cover. *"'Helmets through the Ages: A Detailed History of Headwear,'"* he read aloud. "Ahh, no! There must be some excitement! Some drama! Perhaps some *l'amour*!"

"Let's read an adventure story! One with big, scary monsters!" Chip exclaimed.

"Nothing *too* scary, love," Mrs. Potts said gently. "You don't want to have nightmares."

Belle thought for a moment, her eyes skimming the colorful spines that lined the walls around them. Everyone wanted to read something so *different*. How would she find a story to make everyone happy?

Then Belle had an idea. "Why don't we make up our own bedtime story tonight?" she suggested.

"Our *own* story?" Chip asked, excited.

"Yes." Belle clapped her hands. "We'll go around in a circle and each add a line or two. It'll be fun!"

"A marvelous idea, dear," Mrs. Potts said.

"Magnifique!" Lumiere agreed.

"Quite!" Cogsworth added.

And so the friends gathered around the fire, eager to begin.

Everyone insisted that Belle go first.

"Okay," she agreed. She thought for a moment and then began. "Once upon a time, there was a knight named Sir Allard. Sir Allard was noble and brave. Wherever he went, he rode upon his trusty steed." She smiled, thinking of Philippe.

"Did they fight dragons?" Chip shouted, bouncing eagerly.

Belle laughed at the teacup. "Why don't you go next and tell us?"

"Sir Allard went on *lots* of adventures. He fought big, scary dragons and saved lots of princesses," Chip said. "People came to his castle from all over to ask for his help."

"Ooh, I believe I have something to add," Cogsworth said.

"Wonderful!" Belle said encouragingly.

"Sir Allard's castle was of the *concentric* variety. A vast improvement on the motte-and-bailey castle, the concentric design was a combination of the shell keep and the rectangular keep. It had many lines of defense in the form of multiple stone walls. The stone that was used was particularly interesting . . ."

Cogsworth paused as he noticed Lumiere gesturing for him to finish his part.

"Well, yes, I suppose that was a few lines," Cogsworth sputtered.

"You gave us great details about the setting," Belle said kindly. "Lumiere, would you like to continue?"

"But of course," the candelabrum said. "One day, our hero, Sir Allard, heard about a ferocious dragon. And as all brave knights know, where there is a dragon, there is often a princess. And so, dreaming of rescuing the princess and finding true love, Sir Allard set off to find the dragon. He soon found himself in an enchanted forest—a forest that was so dreadfully dark that he could not see!"

"Ooh!" Mrs. Potts exclaimed. "I know what happens next!"

"As Sir Allard's eyes adjusted, he saw something large resting in the distance," Mrs. Potts said. "It appeared to be the dragon, but the creature didn't look like the knight thought he would. In fact, he looked a bit sad."

"What did he do, Mama?" Chip asked.

"Well, now, I've had my turn, Chip," Mrs. Potts said.

"We've all had our turns!" Cogsworth exclaimed. "Who will finish the tale?"

Suddenly, a cough came from just outside the library door. The group turned to see the Beast standing in the doorway. He had been listening to their story the whole time.

"Hello," Belle called. "Would you care to come in and help us finish the story?"

"No," the Beast said gruffly, turning to leave. "I wouldn't know what to say. . . ."

"Ah, you can do it," Lumiere said.

"It's easy!" Chip added.

"Please," Belle said, motioning for him to sit next to her.

"All right." The
Beast strode over and
sat next to Belle. "Well, I
thought that . . . maybe . . . I
don't know. This is ridiculous,"
he said, fidgeting nervously.

Belle put her hand on his
paw and smiled encouragingly.
He looked at it and then tried
again. "The knight saw that
the dragon was upset . . . and
lonely . . . so Sir Allard talked
to him. And something very
unlikely happened: the two
of them became . . . well . . .
friends. The end."

The room was quiet for a moment. Then everyone began to speak at once.

"*Très bien!*" Lumiere exclaimed.

"Splendid, sir!" Cogsworth cried.

"Very well done, indeed," Mrs. Potts said.

"Yes," Belle said, "that was a wonderful bedtime story"—she smiled at the Beast, who seemed to keep surprising her—"with the most perfect ending."

Tiana's Long Night

IT WAS THE NIGHT before the opening of Tiana's Palace. Tiana had dreamed her whole life of opening her own restaurant. Now that dream was finally coming true—if she could just get everything ready in time!

"Come on, Tiana. You need your rest. Tomorrow is a big day!" said Tiana's mother, Eudora.

"All right, all right, Mama. I'm coming!" Tiana agreed.

Tiana had one foot out the door when, suddenly, she stopped. "I should check on the gumbo one last time . . ." she said. The gumbo was her father's recipe. Tiana wanted it to be her restaurant's star dish.

"I'm sorry, Mama," Tiana said, running back into the kitchen. "I just need this to be perfect!"

Tiana pulled out a spoon and tasted the gumbo. Something was
off. The gumbo was *good*, but it wasn't *perfect*. Tiana couldn't open her
restaurant without perfect gumbo! She set aside the old batch and
started over.

"Looks like it's going to be a long night," she said to herself as she
got to work.

Tiana was an excellent chef, and the gumbo slowly started to come together.

"Mmm-mmm!" Tiana said as she tasted the new batch. "That's more like it."

All the gumbo needed now was some vegetables. Tiana was just about to start mincing them when she had an idea. A welcome banner would be the perfect way to greet her guests.

Leaving the gumbo simmering on the stove, Tiana ran to find some paint and paper. She rolled the paper out in the front entrance and started to make the sign. She was a few letters in when she heard a loud *BANG* coming from the dining room.

"Now, what was *that*?" Tiana asked herself. Putting down her brush, she left the half-finished sign behind and headed into the dining room to find . . . disaster!

A big gust of wind had blown open one of the dining room's doors. The band's sheet music for the grand opening was everywhere!

Tiana hurried to pick up the papers. She wanted to put them back where they belonged, but she didn't know how to read music! What if she put the papers back in the wrong order?

"Well, Tiana, you're in a pickle," she said aloud.

She looked around. She still needed to slice the vegetables for the gumbo and the banner needed to be finished. Setting the pile of papers on a table, she headed back toward the kitchen. The music would have to wait.

Tiana swung the kitchen door open to find the gumbo where she had left it. Next to it was a plate of perfectly minced vegetables!

That's strange, Tiana thought. *Who could have done all that work?*

Tiana was sure that everyone had already gone home for the night. Had she chopped the vegetables herself and forgotten about it?

She shrugged. She didn't have time to dwell on the mystery. There was still a lot of work to do!

With the vegetables prepared, it wasn't long before the gumbo was done. Tiana took one last taste—just right!—before she headed back to finish the sign.

But when Tiana reached the front door, she found that she couldn't finish the sign. It was already done and hanging over the entrance to the restaurant!

I know *I didn't do* that! Tiana thought. *Who could be helping me with all this work?*

Confused, Tiana went back to the dining room. She still had all that sheet music to sort through. But when she looked for the pile she had left on the table, it was gone!

Tiana walked to the stage. The music had been sorted and placed neatly on each musician's stand.

Just then, Tiana heard a happy tune coming from the back deck.

Curious, she opened the door.

Outside, Tiana saw Louis playing his trumpet. Naveen and Eudora were dancing happily to the music.

"Well, well. What do we have here?" Tiana asked the group, laughing.

"I knew as soon as you went back into that kitchen that you would find more work to do!" Tiana's mother said, giving her a big hug. "I wasn't going to let you work through the night all by yourself. I thought you could use some extra hands!"

"Your mother finished your sign," Naveen said. "And you know I love to mince. After all, I *did* learn from the best!" The prince grabbed Tiana around the waist, pulling her into a dance.

"The wind sure made a mess of that sheet music!" Louis added. "Luckily, I know every song. Putting the music in order was easy."

Tiana laughed. "Thank you, everyone! I don't know how I would have gotten everything finished without your help."

"Now there's just one more thing to do," Naveen said.

Tiana looked at him, confused. What was she forgetting?

"We've got to get you home and to bed!" he said. "You've got a big day tomorrow, and you need your rest."

Later, as she climbed into bed, Tiana looked out the window. In the sky, the North Star twinkled down at her.

Tiana remembered wishing on the star years earlier. It had been her dream to open a restaurant with her father. She wished he could be with her to see the dream come true, but she knew he would be proud. And thanks to her friends, the grand opening was sure to be perfect . . . just as it should be.

Mushu's Tale

IT WAS A PEACEFUL night in the Fa household. Mulan helped her grandmother with the dishes. When she'd finished cleaning, Mulan said good night to her family and headed to her room. She had promised Cri-Kee a bedtime story.

Mulan changed into her pajamas and then turned to her friend. "What story would you like to hear tonight, Cri-Kee?"

Before Cri-Kee could answer, their dragon friend Mushu burst into the room. "Did I hear someone ask for a story?"

Mulan nodded. "I was just asking Cri-Kee what kind of story he wanted to hear."

"Ooh, I have the perfect story!" Mushu said excitedly. "Can I tell it?"

Mulan and Cri-Kee both nodded. Mushu's stories *were* always entertaining.

"Excellent!" Mushu said. As Mulan snuggled into bed, Mushu jumped up on the windowsill. Cri-Kee happily nestled on his shoulder.

"It was a dark, snowy evening," Mushu began. "Just like this one. Mulan was just getting into bed when she realized that Cri-Kee's cage was empty.

"Mulan searched the whole house, but there was no sign of the little cricket. Holding her candle to the window, Mulan gasped! Barely visible in the rapidly falling snow was a trail of tiny footprints."

"Hold on," Mulan said, interrupting Mushu's story. "Cri-Kee is so tiny. How would he make tracks in the snow?"

"Shhh," Mushu said. "I am telling a story!"

Mulan nodded and shut her mouth. Mushu was right. It was rude to interrupt.

"Mulan quickly threw on her coat and headed to the ancestors' temple to ask for my help," Mushu continued. "Of course, it didn't take much time to convince me. I would do anything for that lucky bug."

"Unless he's already asleep," Mulan whispered to Cri-Kee. "Trying to wake him up can take forever!"

"I'm going to pretend I didn't hear you," Mushu said. "Anyway, together Mulan and I followed Cri-Kee's trail deep into the woods. The snow continued to fall around us, so hard that we could barely see. We kept following the trail until I accidentally sneezed! Unfortunately, as I am a ferociously fierce fire-breathing dragon, I accidentally melted the snow. We had lost Cri-Kee's trail!"

"Wait a second," Mulan said, interrupting Mushu's story again. "Wouldn't we be able to see the rest of Cri-Kee's trail? You wouldn't have melted *all* the tracks, right?"

Mushu crossed his arms and narrowed his eyes at Mulan. "I was just getting to that part!"

"Sorry, Mushu," Mulan said.

"Just then," Mushu said, "I had a brilliant idea. I tilted my head back and let out a big burst of fire. The flames illuminated the path again, and Mulan was able to spot Cri-Kee's trail.

"We kept following Cri-Kee's trail all the way to a big pile of snow," Mushu said. "But that's where the trail stopped. Mulan and I called for Cri-Kee. We heard a faint chirrup coming from underneath the mound of fallen snow! Mulan and I furiously began scraping away the snow. We dug faster and faster until . . ." Mushu's voice trailed off.

"Until what?" Mulan cried. "What happened next, Mushu?!"

"We uncovered a cave that had been hidden by the snow! Cri-Kee and a little girl from the village were inside," Mushu said. "They were both shivering uncontrollably. Mulan wrapped them in her coat while the little girl explained what had happened. She had been collecting firewood when the snow started. She had stopped in the cave to rest for a minute when suddenly a big pile of snow fell and blocked the entrance. Cri-Kee had heard her cries for help. He was small enough to get inside and keep her company, but he couldn't get them both out!"

"I lit a fire, and we all warmed up before heading home. Everyone was safe and sound. And that's the story of how we found Cri-Kee and rescued the village girl," Mushu finished.

"But how *exactly* did Cri-Kee know that the village girl was in that cave?" Mulan asked, confused. "And why was he out in the storm in the first place?"

"So many questions!" Mushu said, waving his arms in frustration. "It's *just* a story, Mulan."

Mulan smiled at her friend. "It was quite a story."

"It was, wasn't it?" Mushu said. "And telling it has worn me out."

Mushu picked up Cri-Kee and set him on the bed. Then he headed for the door. "Good night, Mulan. Time for sleep."

Mulan agreed. She and Cri-Kee snuggled under the covers, and soon the two drifted off to sleep.

Disney PRINCESS

BRAVE

A Merida and Mum Day

I T WAS A BEAUTIFUL morning in DunBroch. The sun was starting to peek through the mist, and the bright green grass was shining with dew.

In the castle, Merida and her mother, Queen Elinor, were getting ready for their first-ever Merida and Mum day. There was just one problem. The two didn't spend much alone time together. Neither of them knew what to do on their special day!

"Shall we work on our embroidery?" Elinor suggested, leading Merida into a sunny tower.

"Oh . . . if you like," Merida said, trying to sound enthusiastic. She sank into an armchair and picked up some needlework. Then she looked out the window. It was such a nice day.

"I've found this red thread is just perfect for . . ." Elinor paused, noticing that her daughter was distracted. "You know, I could do with a wee bit of fresh air," she said.

Merida's face brightened. "Are you sure?"

"Absolutely," Elinor replied.

Outside, Elinor and Merida walked past Merida's archery field.

"I know!" Merida announced. "I'll teach you how to shoot a bow."

Elinor gave her daughter a weak smile, but Merida didn't notice. She handed her mother a bow and arrow and hopped to the starting line.

"Now, you've just got to line yourself up like so, draw all the way back, and . . . Oh . . . !"

Merida's arrow flew swiftly toward the bull's-eye. But Elinor was not finding archery as easy.

"Mum!" Merida cried as Elinor's arrow hit the ground near her foot. "Are you all right?"

"Yes, dear," Elinor said. "But perhaps archery is not the best mother-daughter activity."

Just then, Elinor spotted the stables in the distance. "I think I know what we can do," she said. "Let's go for a ride!"

As the queen and the princess rode through the beautiful countryside, Elinor called out to her daughter. "Merida! Slow down! I want to show you something."

Merida turned back to find her mother standing in front of a big leafy tree.

"Ehm . . . that's a very nice tree," Merida said. "Quite, ehm, tall."

"This is a rowan tree," Elinor explained. "It is considered the Lady of the Mountain—a protector. Its twigs are hung over doorways to ward off evil spirits."

That got Merida's attention. She loved listening to her mother's tales. "Evil spirits?" she asked.

Elinor glanced at her daughter mischievously. "Shall we collect some twigs for the castle?"

Merida was about to answer when a large scary shadow appeared in the glen. Some monstrous creature was shaking the shrubs surrounding the rowan tree.

"Watch out!" Merida cried, leaping in front of her mother.

Just then, a flash of red curls appeared. It was Merida's brothers, riding a goat!

"Harris, Hubert, Hamish!" Elinor cried. "What are you lot doing here?"

"I thought you were a bogey!" Merida said.

"Well," Elinor said, sighing, "I suppose we'll have to take them back to the castle."

Merida frowned. "Do we have to? Maybe we could just take them with us?"

Elinor leaned in toward Merida. "You're on!"

A wee bit later, Elinor, Merida, and the triplets stopped at a babbling creek. The horses and goat lapped up the cool water.

"Oh, that looks nice and refreshing," Merida said, wading into the creek. Her brothers jumped in after her. Merida turned around to see her mother very delicately sticking a toe in the water.

"Come on in, Mum!" she called. "It feels great."

Elinor hesitated. "Oh, no, I couldn't possibly. . . ."

"You must be so hot," Merida said.

"That may be, but I, well . . ."

Merida looked at her brothers. They knew what to do.

SPLASH! A wave of water hit Elinor.

Merida's mother looked shocked. Then she burst into laughter.

"Oh, no, you don't! I'm going to get you four for that!" she said, joining her children in the creek.

Cooled off from the water, the group decided to do some more exploring. They rode merrily through the forest and soon came across a peaceful meadow. The boys pointed to some large gray stones in the middle of it.

"Oh, yes!" Elinor said. "The old Barry ruins. Let's stop here a moment."

While the boys ran around, playing hide-and-seek in the ruins, Merida studied some carvings etched into one of the stones. "What is that? Can you read it, Mum?"

Elinor peered closely. "If my translation is correct, it says, 'For the noble queen and the brave princess.'" She looked at her daughter warmly. "How about that?"

Merida smiled. Suddenly, she saw her mother's face darken. "Boys!" Elinor called.

The triplets had somehow climbed up one of the rocks. Merida jumped up to collect them.

"I don't know how you do it, watch over all of us," Merida said, handing her squirming brothers down to her mother.

"Well, I've got help," Elinor replied. "They have a good big sister."

All too soon, the sun began to set.

"I think it's time to go home," Elinor said.

As the group rode, they spotted some fireflies dancing in the meadow.

"Fireflies are the fairies' messengers," Elinor explained. "We just have to whisper our wishes to them. Shall we?"

Merida grinned and hopped off her horse. As the boys tried to catch the bright, buzzing bugs, mother and daughter whispered their deepest wishes.

Later, back at the castle, Merida stopped her mother. "What did you wish for?" she asked.

"We're not supposed to say, or it won't come true," Elinor said.

Merida shrugged. "I wished to have more Merida and Mum days."

Elinor pulled her daughter into a hug. "Me too," she whispered.

Merida smiled. She knew that was one wish that would come true.

POCAHONTAS

Lost and Found

THE LAST RAYS OF the setting sun shone down on Pocahontas as she lay daydreaming in her canoe. Beside her, Meeko the raccoon snored softly. Flit the hummingbird sat on the edge of the canoe, his head tucked under his wing. As the gentle current slowly pulled the trio down the river, Pocahontas thought about all that had happened that day and all she hoped would happen in the next.

Suddenly, she heard a familiar voice calling her name. "Pocahontas! Pocahontas!" Standing on the riverbank was Nakoma, Pocahontas's best friend.

Pocahontas sat up in her canoe. "Nakoma! Over here!" she said, waving her arm over her head.

"There you are," Nakoma said. "Your father sent me to bring everyone back to the village. A bad storm is coming!"

Pocahontas looked up at the sky. She could see a few dark clouds on the horizon, but they looked far away.

"I'll meet you there!" she called as she lay back in her canoe.

Nakoma started to argue, but she knew better. And she still had more people to find. With one last look at her friend, she turned around and headed back into the forest.

Before long, the gentle motion of the boat had lulled Pocahontas, Meeko, and Flit to sleep. All around them, the wind picked up and the river began to get choppy. Suddenly, a huge wave broke over the side of the canoe, waking the friends!

Pocahontas gasped. The storm must have nearly reached the river!

Pocahontas picked up her paddle and began to row. Finally, with Meeko's help, she managed to get to shore.

"Come on!"
Pocahontas called to
Meeko and Flit. "We
have to get home
before it starts to rain."

Pocahontas looked
up at the sky. The sun
had set while she slept.
Now it was impossible to tell
how close the storm was. But if the
strong winds were any sign, the rain wouldn't be far off.

Suddenly, a particularly strong gust swept through the woods. Flit's
little wings weren't big enough to fight against it, and he blew backward.
Luckily, Meeko was there to catch him.

"Don't worry—we're almost there!" Pocahontas called over her
shoulder.

In the village, Pocahontas found everyone working hard to prepare for the storm. She hurried over to help.

Pocahontas gathered basket after basket of corn. When they were all together, she secured a hide over them to keep the food dry. Pocahontas was just checking the strength of the covering when the first drop of rain fell on her head. She gave the rope one more tug and then ran into her father's tent. As she stepped inside, the clouds burst open and it began to pour.

"Daughter, there you are!" Chief Powhatan said, wrapping Pocahontas in a hug. "I feared Nakoma would not find you in time. I should have trusted that she knows your ways well."

"I'm sorry, Father," Pocahontas said. "Nakoma tried to make me come back, but I didn't listen."

Pocahontas paused. She didn't remember seeing her friend in the village.

"Father, do you know where Nakoma *is*?" she asked.

The chief looked at his daughter, concerned. "I thought she was with you," he said.

Pocahontas heard the storm raging outside. If Nakoma was still out there, she could be hurt or in trouble.

"I have to go look for her!" Pocahontas told her father.

Before Chief Powhatan could stop her, Pocahontas ran back outside—right into the middle of the storm!

"Nakoma! Nakoma!" Pocahontas shouted as she sprinted back toward the river. Her friend had to be there somewhere. But the rain was too heavy. Pocahontas could barely see in front of her face! She had to hold on tight to the trees to keep from being blown away.

Pocahontas called out again. The storm was so loud that she didn't
know if her friend could even hear her!

Pocahontas knew that she should return to the safety of her village,
but she had to find her best friend! Determined, she pressed on.

Pocahontas had almost reached the river's edge when, suddenly, she heard something. Cupping a hand to her ear, she tried to concentrate on the sound. It was faint, but it sounded like someone calling her name!

"Nakoma—is that you?" Pocahontas called.

"Pocahontas! Where are you?" her friend called back.

"Keep yelling, Nakoma! I'll find you!" Pocahontas shouted.

Pocahontas followed the sound of her friend's voice. At last, she found her huddled against a rock.

"Pocahontas! I can't believe you found me in this terrible storm. I was so focused on finding everyone else and telling them to get to safety that I lost track of time. By the time I turned back, the storm had started and I got lost in the rain and wind!"

"It's okay, Nakoma!" Pocahontas said, taking Nakoma's hand. "We'll get home together. I think the storm came in from the west. If we just push against the wind, we should be heading east! That's the way back to the village."

Together, the friends headed back into the storm. Although it was still very dark and windy, the storm didn't seem as bad now that Pocahontas had found Nakoma.

Finally, Pocahontas and Nakoma reached Chief Powhatan's tent. Pocahontas's father was relieved to see them and handed the girls warm blankets.

Outside, the storm continued to rage. But inside, Pocahontas and Nakoma were dry and happy. The two huddled by the fire, listening to Chief Powhatan tell stories about the tribe's past and future, until at last they drifted to sleep, tired from the night's adventure.

Cinderella
A Nighttime Stroll

"CINDERELLY! CINDERELLY!" GUS YELLED, running into Cinderella's room. "There's a new mouse in the barn! Her name is Greta. Can she stay with us?"

Cinderella smiled at her mouse friend. "Of course!" she said. "There's always room here for one more!"

Cinderella loved her mouse friends. She had rescued them from her stepmother's cat, Lucifer, before she met the Prince. Now they lived with her in the palace.

Cinderella and the mice got to work. They wanted to make their new friend feel right at home!

The mice built a tiny bed for Greta and stuffed a mouse-sized mattress with dandelion fluff from the palace lawn. Meanwhile, Cinderella sewed Greta some new clothes, and Gus made a nightstand out of a spool of thread.

"Greta will sleep like a baby mouse!" Gus said, placing a small vase of flowers on the nightstand.

Gus couldn't wait to introduce his new friend to Cinderella!

"Greta!" Gus cried. "This is Cinderelly!"

The princess knelt to shake Greta's tiny paw with her pinkie finger. "You're very welcome here," the princess said. "You must be hungry."

Greta patted her tummy and nodded.

Cinderella smiled at her new mouse friend. "Well, why don't we get you dressed, and then we'll have a nice, filling dinner!"

While the mice had been making Greta's bed, Cinderella's bird friends had prepared a huge welcome feast. There was a baby-lettuce salad, grilled cheese soup with tiny toast corners, and every kind of nut the palace kitchen stocked.

Greta happily dug in to the food while the mice asked her all sorts of questions. Soon Gus noticed Greta's eyelids drooping. Taking her by the paw, he showed her to her new bed.

"Oh!" Greta said, clapping in delight. "Such a snug bed! Thank you! Thank you!"

Greta climbed into her bed and was soon fast asleep, snoring softly into her dandelion pillow.

Later that night, a shadowy
figure marched down a path in
the royal garden.

"Halt!" one of the watchmen
called. "Who goes there?"

The guard knelt down and
peered into the shadowy lane.
"Why, it's one of Her Highness's
mouse friends!" he said.

Greta rubbed her eyes and
looked around. "Where am I?"
she asked, confused.

The guard smiled and told
Greta that she was in the
garden. Then he walked her
back to the palace.

The next morning, Greta told her new friends all about her nighttime adventure. "It was so strange!" she said. "One moment I was in bed, all cozy and snug, having the nicest dream. . . ."

"And then-a what happened?" Jaq asked.

"I woke up in the garden!" Greta exclaimed. "In my nightgown! With no idea how I'd gotten there!"

The mice gasped.

"I've never sleepwalked before, not ever!" Greta said, taking a bite of a blueberry.

Everyone agreed that Greta's sleepwalking was likely a one-time thing. She was probably just getting used to her new bed.

"I'm sure it won't happen again," Greta agreed cheerfully.

That night, Greta went to bed confident that she'd stay put until morning. A few hours later, though, she woke up at the palace gates with no memory of how she'd gotten there!

Then, the night after that, she marched right through the gates and into the street.

"Rats," Greta said as a kind villager walked her back to the palace.

Over the next few days, Cinderella and her mouse friends did everything they could to help Greta.

Jaq tried giving her a glass of warm milk before bed. "Always helps-a me sleep tight!" he said. But that night, Greta woke up in the middle of the village.

Gus tried putting noisy crumpled paper around Greta's bed, but she marched right through it without blinking an eye.

Cinderella tried putting a mouse-sized gate at the front door, but Greta picked the lock and waltzed right out of the palace . . . without waking up!

"I didn't even know I *could* pick locks!" Greta said. "You learn something new every day!"

"Or every night," Gus agreed.

No matter how hard Cinderella and her friends tried to keep Greta inside the palace, nothing worked. Every night she woke up farther and farther away. Finally, very early one morning, Greta woke up with sore feet in a village she didn't recognize. She'd never been that far from the palace before. She couldn't even see it on the horizon.

"Where *am* I?" the little mouse wondered out loud as she walked the streets. The town she'd sleepwalked into was tiny and quiet. Everyone was still asleep.

Suddenly, Greta stopped. The most glorious smell was wafting out of a little shop.

"A cheese shop!" Greta exclaimed. The glorious smell that practically had her floating closer to the door was *cheese*. But not just any cheese.

"I've never smelled a cheese like that," Greta murmured. It was stinky and rich, and she was sure it would taste amazing.

Greta raced all the way back to the palace.

"I solved the mystery!" she said, bursting through the door.

Greta explained her latest adventure to her friends. "My nose has been leading me to that cheese shop every night!" she said. "It just took me a while to get there."

Everyone was curious about the amazing cheese. What could smell so wonderful that it made Greta sleepwalk all the way to the next village?

So, shortly after breakfast, Cinderella summoned the royal coach. Soon she and her mouse friends were on their way to the countryside.

"There it is!" Greta squeaked, pointing to the shop.

The coach pulled to a stop, and the friends climbed out.

The humble cheese shop owner was very surprised to find himself with none other than the royal princess and a handful of mice as his first customers of the day.

It took Greta only a few seconds of sniffing around to identify the stinky cheese she'd been sleepwalking toward. "It's this one!" she said.

The shop owner happily gave Greta a sample.

"Oh, it's *glorious*!" Greta said. "It's like sunrise and sunset and smelly feet all rolled into one!"

Cinderella was glad her new friend had found something she enjoyed so much. With a wink at the shop owner, she bought an entire wheel of the cheese for her little friend.

That night, Greta had a wonderful bedtime snack: several tiny crackers smeared with her new favorite cheese.

"Yum!" she said. "That really hit the spot."

Then, her tummy full, she snuggled into bed—where she stayed all night.

THE LITTLE MERMAID
The Ghost Lights

LATE ONE NIGHT, ARIEL awoke to the sound of coughing. Her sister Andrina was sick.

Ariel swam over to her sister. "Is there anything I can do to help?" she whispered, careful not to wake the others. "Maybe get some night-lily tea?"

Everyone knew that freshly picked night lily was the best cure for a bad cold.

"You can't," croaked Andrina. "The doctor hasn't been able to gather night lily for days. They say the flowers are guarded . . . by a *ghost*!"

Ariel wasn't afraid of ghosts. Her sister needed that medicine, and she was going to get it for her!

Sneaking out of her room, Ariel went to find Flounder. Together, they took off to gather night lilies.

As they neared the edge of the kingdom, Ariel and Flounder saw a group of guards peering into the dark ocean.

"What are they looking at?" Flounder asked.

"Shhh, they'll hear you!" whispered Ariel.

Ariel wasn't supposed to leave the kingdom at night. If the guards saw her, they would make her go home!

Suddenly, a group of small blue lights moved in the darkness!

"There they are," one guard said.

"The ghost lights! Let's go take a look," said another guard.

"No, never get close to the ghost lights!" said the first guard. "They'll make you follow them, and you'll be lost forever."

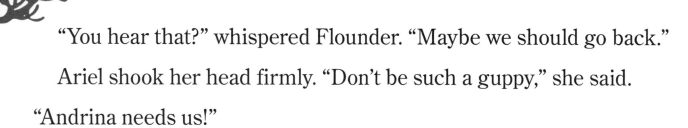

"You hear that?" whispered Flounder. "Maybe we should go back."

Ariel shook her head firmly. "Don't be such a guppy," she said.

"Andrina needs us!"

Ariel pulled Flounder along by the fin, and they snuck past the guards.

The lights bobbed and danced as they got closer. "Wh-wh-what do you think it is?" asked Flounder. "Is it an octopus?"

The lights moved and changed shape.

"It's a shark!" Flounder cried. The little fish covered his eyes with his fins.

Ariel laughed. "Don't be silly. Sharks don't glow in the dark! But there's definitely *something* strange going on. Come on, let's take a closer look."

As they approached the lights, Ariel and Flounder saw that they weren't one big creature but a whole school of fish! Each fish was covered in glowing blue spots. Below them was a patch of night lilies!

"There they are!" Ariel shouted. "Come on, let's get them and go home."

Ariel and Flounder were sneaking toward the flowers when a fish swam up to them. "Can you help us?" it cried.

"Are you going to make us follow you?" Flounder asked the fish in a shaky voice. "We don't want to be lost forever!"

"What?" asked the fish. "We're the ones who are lost! We're glowing toadfish. We belong near the shore. We've tried and tried to find our way back, but we always end up by these flowers."

Ariel looked at the glowing blue fish. Then she looked at the glowing blue flowers.

"I know how to help!" she said. "Follow me."

Ariel, Flounder, and the school of fish swam to the surface of the ocean.

"From far away, the night lilies look like you," Ariel explained. "That's why you keep swimming toward them. You think they're your family!" She pointed up to the night sky. "Just follow that bright star, and you'll find the shore."

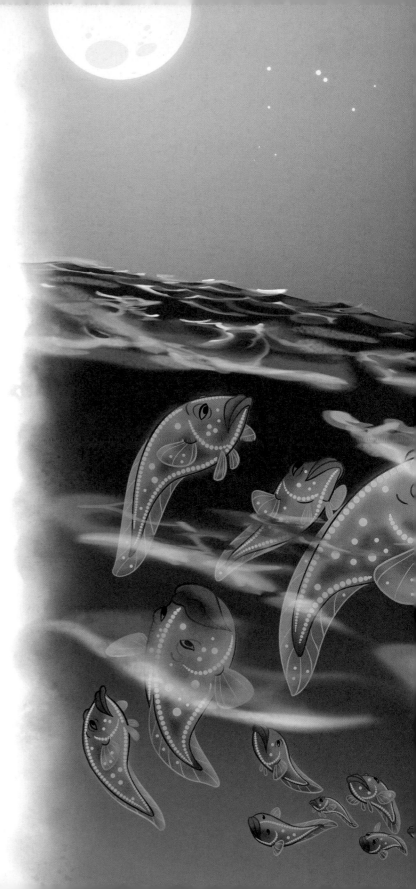

The fish spun around and around Ariel in thanks. Then they swam off.

Ariel and Flounder dove down to the night-lily field. They picked as many flowers as they could carry.

A few minutes later, the border guards saw what looked like two bright blue eyes racing out of the darkness at them!

"It's the ghost lights!" they yelled.

"Don't worry! It's just me and Flounder," called Ariel.

The guards laughed in relief. "Princess," said one guard, "you shouldn't be out past the border in the dark."

"I'm not afraid of the dark—or ghost stories," replied Ariel. "Plus my sister needs this medicine."

Ariel and Flounder rushed to the palace with the glowing flowers. In no time, the doctor had made a fresh batch of night-lily tea.

Ariel brought the tea to her sister. Soon Andrina felt so much better that she couldn't stop talking. She told anyone who would listen just how brave Ariel was—and how she had saved the day!

Tangled

Rapunzel's Campout

SPRING HAD FINALLY ARRIVED in Corona. The air was full of the sweet smell of flowers and the chirping of returning birds.

All winter long, Rapunzel had been cooped up inside. She and her father had organized the royal ledgers. She and her mother had picked new pieces of art for the royal gallery. And she had helped the kingdom's planners prepare for the summer festival.

Now, as she made her way through the village, Rapunzel began to skip. She enjoyed being helpful, but with the weather turning warm, she wanted adventure! She was ready to get outside and do something exciting.

Rapunzel was turning a corner when she crashed into an older woman. "Oh!" she said, startled. "I'm so very sorry."

"No need to apologize," the woman said with a smile. She was holding on to a small donkey hitched to a cart full of flowers. "I've just arrived in the village. I'm not used to so much commotion."

Rapunzel tilted her head. "Do you not live here?" she asked.

The woman shook her head. "I live wherever my feet take me," she explained. "My roof is the stars and my floor, the green grass."

As Rapunzel watched the woman go on her way, she had an idea. Sleeping under the stars sounded like just the sort of grand adventure she was looking for!

Rapunzel couldn't wait to invite her friends and family. She was sure they would be as excited as she was!

There was just one problem: no one could go with her.

Rapunzel's parents were busy planning a royal dinner. "Have fun, dear," the Queen said as she looked over the invitations.

"Be careful of wild animals!" the King added, studying the ice sculptures the royal carver had created.

Eugene was busy, too. He was getting ready for a joust. "Sorry, Rapunzel," he said. "I need all the practice I can get."

Eugene let out a shout as his horse spooked and jumped to the side, nearly tossing him to the ground. Regaining control, he added, "But be on the lookout for bears. I hear they're hungry this time of year."

Rapunzel sighed. At least she had her trusty friend Pascal to keep her company. "We'll have a good time—just the two of us. Right?"

Pascal blinked his big round eyes and flicked out his long tongue.

Rapunzel took that as a yes. "Come on," she said. "Let's go get some food."

Rapunzel and Pascal headed to the royal kitchen to pack a basket of food. Rapunzel thought a bit of cheese, a loaf of bread, and some fruit would be just right.

Just as she was reaching for the bread, the chef came in. Eager to help the princess, she insisted on packing the basket herself.

By the time Rapunzel left the kitchen, she had two baskets overflowing with food she knew she would never eat.

Next Rapunzel went to pack a small bag. But when she got to her room, she found her mother's maid putting away the laundry. Before she knew it, Rapunzel had two small bags and a trunk full of dresses.

"But I'm just going for one night," she protested as the maid closed the trunk. "I won't need any of these things."

The maid just shook her head and ordered a valet to take everything downstairs.

Finally, her cart loaded with bags, Rapunzel set off. "We'd better get moving, Pascal," she told the chameleon. "We need to find a place to set up camp before it gets dark."

As Rapunzel drove the cart through the countryside, she swiveled her head left and right. At last, she came upon a large patch of clear ground beside a stream. Branches from a large willow tree provided just enough shade, and the trunk was a good place to rest her back. It was perfect.

Rapunzel wasted no time. She unhooked the horse from the wagon and then set about collecting firewood. In no time, she had a pile of branches.

Rapunzel stacked the branches in a circle. Then, rubbing two pieces of wood together, she got a small fire going. It was just big enough to cook some food and keep her warm.

Rapunzel looked at the baskets of food the chef had prepared. Then she reached into her bag, pulled out a net, and marched into the stream. Soon she had caught three fish for dinner!

Rapunzel smiled. She was sure making dinner herself would be more satisfying than just eating what the chef had sent with her.

As the sun set, Rapunzel prepared her fish and cooked them over the fire. She had just taken her first bite when she heard a rustling noise behind her. Rapunzel jumped to her feet. Her father's warning echoed in her mind.

She heard the noise again.

Taking a deep breath, Rapunzel stepped away from the campfire.

The sound grew louder. It was coming from behind a large bush. Very carefully, Rapunzel walked up to the bush and peered through the branches.

Her eyes narrowed. Her nostrils flared. And then she burst out laughing.

It was nothing but a small gray squirrel.

"Now don't I feel silly?" Rapunzel said to Pascal.

Pascal nodded. Then he blinked three times.

"I know," Rapunzel answered. "It was just a squirrel, but it *could* have been a bear. I need to be better prepared."

Rapunzel knew just what to do. She grabbed a shovel and dug a large hole behind her camp. Then she covered it up with several green and brown dresses from her trunk.

Next she needed bait. Digging through the chef's baskets, she pulled out a slab of meat. Using her net, she tied the meat to a tree branch hanging above the hole. If any animal tried to grab the meat, it would fall into the hole!

Feeling much better, Rapunzel went back to relaxing by the fire. Then she heard a thud and a loud groan. Something had fallen into her trap!

Running over, Rapunzel prepared herself to find a bear. But to her surprise, she found Eugene. He lay at the bottom of the hole, covered in dirt.

"Eugene! What are you doing here?" Rapunzel asked.

"I came to surprise you!" Eugene answered. "But *I'm* the one who got surprised."

Laughing, Rapunzel helped Eugene out of the hole. "Sorry! But you *were* the one who told me about bears!" she said, smiling.

"I should have known you would be fine on your own," Eugene said.

Rapunzel nodded. "I am," she agreed. "But I'm glad you're here. A camping trip is always more fun when you have stories to share, and after today, I have plenty of those!"

The Best-Friend Sleepover

"COME ON, TIA. IT'S one day!" Charlotte said. "Surely you can be away from the restaurant for *one day*!"

Tiana sighed. For days Charlotte had been trying to talk her into going on a shopping trip. The problem was Tiana just had too much to do at her restaurant. She barely had time to sit down, much less take a whole day off!

"Please! Pretty please! With powdered sugar on top?" Charlotte pleaded.

Tiana looked around the kitchen. She still had to finish the gumbo, make the corn bread, and prepare that night's special dish.

"I'm sorry, Lottie," she said, shaking her head. "Tiana's Palace needs me. I don't have time to watch you try on a hundred dresses. Making sure everything here runs smoothly is just too important."

Tiana turned and went back to chopping carrots. "Maybe next week," she said. "Or the week after that."

Charlotte crossed her arms and pouted. "All you think about is your restaurant," she said. "What about your friends? This is *important*! I need a new dress for Big Daddy's gala."

"Lottie," Tiana began, "I told you—"

"Fine!" Charlotte said, cutting her off. "If that's how you feel, I'll go by myself. But see if I'm around the next time *you* need help!"

With a stomp, Charlotte turned around and stormed out of the kitchen, slamming the door behind her on the way out.

That afternoon, Charlotte went to her favorite boutique. She tried on every dress they had.

But shopping for a dress just wasn't the same without her best friend. With no one to model for, her favorite pastime just wasn't any *fun*.

Meanwhile, Tiana finished making the gumbo. And she made the corn bread. And she prepared the night's special.

Tiana looked at the pile of dirty dishes and sighed. Dishes were her least favorite part of working in the kitchen. But most nights she had Lottie to talk to while she worked. Listening to her best friend's excited chatter always seemed to make the cleanup go faster. Without her, the job seemed to drag on and on.

That night, as Tiana got ready for bed, she looked out the window. If she had learned anything from her father, it was the importance of friends and family.

Tiana sighed. The restaurant was important, but not as important as Lottie. She knew she had to find a way to make up with her best friend.

Over at the LaBouff estate, Charlotte grumbled. And she complained. But most of all, she missed Tiana. Maybe she had taken things too far when she stormed out of Tiana's Palace. After all, the restaurant had been Tiana's dream for as long as Charlotte could remember. And making sure it ran smoothly *was* important.

Lottie knew she had to find a way to make up with her best friend.

The next morning, Tiana heard a noise coming from the kitchen. Then she smelled something burning! Flinging open the door, she found Charlotte standing over a pot of boiling oil and burned beignets.

"Lottie!" Tiana said. "What are you doing?"

Just then, Tiana noticed a tear sliding down Charlotte's cheek.

"I just wanted to help," Charlotte explained. "I felt bad about yesterday, and I thought maybe I could make it up to you. But now I've ruined everything!"

Tiana sighed and hugged Charlotte. "I'm sorry, too. I should have remembered that some things are more important than my restaurant. And you're right at the top of that list!"

Tiana looked around the kitchen. "You were right, Lottie," she continued. "This place can run without me for a day. And I know just what we need. A good old-fashioned Tiana-and-Charlotte day!"

"Oh, Tia, really?" Charlotte asked. "That sounds wonderful!"

Tiana and Charlotte cleaned up the mess in the kitchen. Then Tiana showed her best friend how to make beignets—the right way!

In no time, Charlotte was rolling out the dough and frying up perfect beignets! "Now that's more like it!" she cried, examining her handiwork.

Next the two went
shopping. Charlotte
tried on dress after
dress. All the gowns
that had seemed
drab and boring the
day before seemed
perfect now.

Soon Charlotte
had found not one,
not two, but *three*
dresses for Big
Daddy's gala!

She even helped
Tiana pick out the
perfect gown.

That night, Tiana lay on Charlotte's bed. "What are you doing, Lottie?" she called to her best friend. "I'm exhausted. Let's go to bed!"

"I'm looking for . . ." Charlotte began, then trailed off. "Where is it? Ah!" Charlotte poked her head out of the closet. "This!" she said, holding up a book.

Tiana smiled. It was the book her mother had read to them as children. "What a perfect way to end our day," she said.

Charlotte nodded and scrambled onto the bed next to Tiana. Then, opening the book, the two snuggled up to read the bedtime story together.

THE LITTLE MERMAID
Ariel's Night Lights

Princess Ariel loved living on land. For so long, she had watched the human world from a distance. But now, she actually got to learn about it up close!

One evening, Ariel and Prince Eric decided to eat dessert on their balcony. To Eric, it was a normal, peaceful night. But for Ariel, nighttime on land was full of fascinating new sights.

"Nighttime is so different here than it is under the sea," Ariel told
Eric.

"What do you mean?" Eric asked.

Ariel smiled. "Beneath the waves, the only lights we have are glowing
jellyfish and the little bit of moonlight that seeps down from the surface,"
she explained. "But here on land you have fire that you can use to light
up the night!"

Eric smiled at Ariel. "Fire isn't the only thing on land that lights the night," he said. "I know something else I think you'll love."

Eric put out the torches, leaving the balcony in darkness—but not total darkness. Ariel's eyes widened as she spotted a bunch of small bright sparks zipping through the air around them. With the torches lit, she hadn't been able to see them.

"What are they?" she exclaimed. "They're a lot smaller than the jellyfish we had under the sea."

Prince Eric chuckled. "They're called fireflies," he said. He caught one and then opened his hand so Ariel could look at it. "See? Their bodies light up."

Ariel carefully reached for the firefly, gasping in delight as it lit up again. The firefly flew out of Eric's hand. Soon it was lost among dozens of its friends.

"They're lovely," Ariel said. "They move through the air as easily as fish through the water."

"Does everything here remind you of fish?" Eric teased gently.

Ariel laughed. "Not everything," she replied. "Actually, these fireflies remind me much more of something else."

Ariel pointed upward. Countless tiny points of light twinkled far overhead.

"The stars?" Eric guessed.

"Yes," Ariel said. "Fireflies look as if they could be tiny stars that have come to live on land—just like I did!"

Eric raised his eyebrows. "I never thought of it that way."

"It's too bad there's so much light coming from the palace," Ariel said. "It makes it hard to see all the stars."

"What do you mean?" Eric said. "There are plenty of stars out tonight."

"Not as many as I could see when I used to sneak up to the surface," Ariel told him. "I suppose it's easier to see them out there because it's so much darker."

"I suppose you're right," Eric agreed. "Even if I put out every torch in the palace, there would still be light coming from the village and the farms nearby."

Ariel grabbed his hand. "Then let's go where there are no villages and no farms," she said. "Can we, please? I want to see the stars—all of them!"

Eric looked surprised, but he nodded. "I'll summon a carriage."

Soon the carriage arrived. Eric and Ariel climbed aboard and rode out through the palace gates. Their carriage traveled through the village and along a windy path up into the rolling countryside. They passed several farms, with animals sleeping in the fields. The farther they traveled from the lights of the village, the darker the world around them grew. Finally, the carriage came to a stop at the top of the largest hill.

Hopping out of the carriage, Ariel looked around. Far, far below, she could just make out the faint glow of the palace on the horizon. A few lights shone in the houses in the village. But their light didn't reach that far up into the hills.

Ariel turned slowly in circles, looking up at the night sky. It seemed there were even more stars to see here than when she had looked at the sky from the ocean.

"Oh, Eric. This is perfect!" she said.

Ariel and Eric walked
through the soft grass.
Eric laid out a blanket.

Ariel sat down,
turning her eyes toward
the sky. "Look," she told
Eric. "Now we can see all the
stars."

Eric lay back, crossing
his arms behind his head
and taking in the view of the
night sky. "You were right,
Ariel," he said. "I've never
seen so many stars!
There are too many to
count!"

Ariel gazed upward. "It's nice to be able to look at the stars," she said. "When I lived under the sea, I wasn't supposed to visit the surface. So I never really got to study the sky. Doesn't that group of stars over there look like a ship?"

"It does!" Eric said. "And those stars could be a dog, and over there I think I can see a trident, like the one your father carries. . . ."

Ariel pointed at another set of stars. "Those look like my friend Sebastian!" she said.

Ariel and Eric laughed as they pointed out different shapes in the stars. Suddenly, one of the stars seemed to fall from the sky! Ariel gasped.

"Did you see that?" she cried. "That bright star there—it's moving! Look! There's another one!"

"Those aren't stars," Eric told her. "It must be a meteor shower."

Ariel watched the falling meteors. "They're beautiful," she said. "I guess I was right after all."

Eric looked over at her. "You were right about what?"

Ariel smiled as the twinkling stars reflected in her eyes. "The stars really *do* want to come down to land!"

Sleeping Beauty

Briar Rose to the Rescue

"OH, DRAT," FLORA SAID, peering into the fireplace. "We're out of wood!"

"No wood?" Merryweather asked, alarmed. "But how will we stay warm overnight? Why, with no fire, we'll freeze!"

Briar Rose smiled at her aunt. She loved her dearly, but Merryweather certainly had a flair for the dramatic.

"I'll go fetch some more," Briar Rose offered. Then, putting on her cloak, she stepped out of the cottage. "I'll be right back!" she called.

Briar Rose didn't have to go far to find wood. By the time she had taken a few steps into the forest, her arms were full of branches. But as she turned to go home, Briar Rose heard a noise.

"Hoo! Hoo!"

Briar Rose spun around to see her friend the owl perched on a tree branch.

"Why, hello there," Briar Rose called back. "How are you this evening?"

"Hoo! Hoo!" the owl called again. He flapped his wings frantically and hopped up and down on the branch. Then, with one more hoot, he flew deeper into the forest.

Briar Rose frowned. Her animal friends were usually quite calm. It was not like the owl to seem so upset. She hoped nothing was wrong.

Setting down the pile of branches she had collected, she followed the owl deep into the woods.

The owl landed on a large oak tree. Briar Rose knew that a family of rabbits lived inside. Her heart pounded. "Is something wrong with the bunnies?" she asked.

Briar Rose knelt down and looked into the hollow tree trunk. The mother rabbit was there, anxiously fussing over her babies.

"One . . . two . . ." Briar Rose counted. "Where is the third bunny? There should be one more here!"

Now Briar Rose knew why the owl had seemed so upset. A baby bunny was missing!

"Don't worry. I'll find him," Briar Rose promised. "And you'll help me, won't you, owl?"

"Hoo! Hoo!" the owl agreed.

Briar Rose stood up and looked at the forest trail. The sky was growing dark, but she could just make out tiny paw prints on the ground.

"Look!" she said, pointing at the trail. "He went that way. Let's go!"

Briar Rose followed the trail, with the owl flying close behind. But the deeper she got into the woods, the more the trees blocked the moonlight. "Soon I won't be able to see a thing!" she said.

As she spoke, a cloud of fireflies flew up to her. They blinked on and off, lighting up the path. Briar Rose smiled, surprised. "Oh! Thank you!" she said. "That's *much* better."

The paw prints led to a stream and then disappeared.

"Hmmm," Briar Rose said. "The little guy must have hopped across the stream on those rocks."

Briar Rose started to step on the nearest rock. But it wasn't a rock. It was a turtle shell! A sleepy turtle poked her head out of the water.

"Oh, my!" Briar Rose said, pulling her foot back. "I'm so sorry. I didn't mean to step on you. I was just trying to get across the stream. Your shell looked like a stone. Are there any more of you in the water?"

At the commotion, four more sleepy turtles popped their heads up and looked around.

"I'm sorry to wake you," Briar Rose said, "but I don't want to step on you by mistake!" Briar Rose bent down and peered at the turtles' shells. Now that she knew what she was looking for, she could see the difference between the turtles and the rocks.

"Thank you," she said as she carefully stepped across the rocks. "You can go back to sleep now."

On the other side of the stream, Briar Rose spotted the bunny's paw prints. All around her, the sounds of the forest filled the air. Crickets chirped. Tiny wood mice scurried through the pine needles. Bats flapped their wings as they swept through the trees. But Briar Rose barely noticed. She was too focused on finding the bunny.

Suddenly, a pair of yellow eyes appeared. Frightened, the fireflies fled. The owl let out a startled hoot. But Briar Rose stood tall.

"Who's there?" she asked.

A small red fox trotted out of the bushes.

Briar Rose smiled. "Hello there!" she said. Briar Rose pointed to the trail of footprints. It had now grown so dark that she could barely see them. "I'm looking for a lost bunny. Have you seen him?"

The fox looked at Briar Rose, confused. Then she began to sniff the ground. A moment later, she turned and walked away.

Briar Rose quickly set off after the fox.

"Hoo! Hoo!" Suddenly, the owl let out a warning cry and flew in front of Briar Rose. She stopped and looked down—right at the edge of a cliff! The fox was making her way across a fallen tree to get to the other side. But Briar Rose had nearly stepped over the edge!

"Thank you, owl," Briar Rose said. "It's a good thing that you can see so well at night!"

Then, following the fox's lead, she carefully walked across the fallen tree.

The fox led Briar Rose to the edge of the forest. Ahead she could see a cottage with a big vegetable garden.

"Thank you," Briar Rose called out to her new friend. But the fox had already disappeared back into the woods.

Stepping out of the forest, Briar Rose headed toward the cottage. The moon shone brightly overhead, and she could easily see the missing bunny sleeping happily in a patch of lettuce.

Laughing softly, Briar Rose picked up the sleeping bunny and made her way back over the fallen tree, across the stream, and to the hollow tree that was home to the family of rabbits.

"Here you are," Briar Rose said, placing the bunny inside the hollow. "Safe and sound."

The sleeping bunny snuggled up next to his brother and sister, wiggling slightly as his mother licked him all over.

Briar Rose smiled at the rabbits. Then she yawned. "Oh, my, I'm getting very sleepy, too! I need to get back to the cottage."

Gathering her firewood, Briar Rose returned to the cottage, where the three anxious fairies were waiting for her.

"Where were you?" Flora asked.

"We were so worried about you!" Fauna exclaimed.

"We went to look for you, but all we could find was an abandoned pile of twigs," Merryweather said. "We thought someone had kidnapped you!"

"I'm sorry," Briar Rose said. "It was an emergency. Besides, who would want to hurt *me*?"

"Now, now, Merryweather, she's just fine," Fauna said. Then, turning to Briar Rose, she added, "How about some cake and a nice hot cup of tea, and you can tell us everything that happened?"

So Briar Rose and her aunts settled in for the night, and the girl told them all about her adventure.

Beauty and the Beast

Star Stories

TWILIGHT WAS FALLING AS Belle and Chip strolled through the castle gardens.

"Look," Belle said, pointing at the sky. "There's Draco the dragon."

"A dragon?" Chip gasped, looking around. "Where?"

"It's not a *real* dragon," Belle replied. "It's a constellation."

Chip scrunched up his face in confusion. "A consta-what?"

"A constellation," Belle repeated. "It's a group of stars that look like a picture." Belle traced the air with her finger, outlining the image of Draco the dragon. "See? Those stars look like a dragon."

Chip jumped up and down in excitement. "I see it! I see Draco!"

Then he stopped. "How many other constellations are there up there?" he asked Belle. "How did people find them?"

Belle smiled. "Follow me. I know where we can learn about them!"

In the library, Belle found a book about constellations. "'Long ago, people searched the stars for hidden pictures,'" she read aloud. "'These star pictures became known as constellations. The constellations inspired many stories, some of which we still tell today.'"

"What kind of stories?" Chip wondered.

"Sometimes the stories are about great adventures," Belle replied. "Other times they explain how something extraordinary happened." She turned the page. "Look! There's a map of the night sky showing all the different constellations."

Chip peered at the book. "Let's go outside and find them!" he shouted, hopping down from the table and bouncing toward the door.

Belle followed Chip. But when they got outside, the sky was dark and cloudy.

"I'm sorry, Chip," she said. "It's too cloudy to see constellations tonight."

"No fair," Chip said sadly. "I *really* wanted to see the constellations."

Chip looked disappointed. Belle wanted to help him feel better, but how? Suddenly, she had an idea. "Maybe," she began, "we could make our own constellation! We could hang it in the library and come up with a story to go with it!"

"Yeah!" Chip cheered. "Let's do it!"

"First we'll need something shiny and sparkly for the stars," Belle said thoughtfully. "I know just who to ask."

Belle led Chip upstairs to her bedroom, where the Wardrobe was setting out a dress for her to wear the next day.

"You two look like you're up to something," the Wardrobe said.

"We're working on a project—" Belle began. Before she could finish, Chip interrupted her.

"But we can't tell you what it is. It's a surprise!" he exclaimed. "Do you have anything sparkly or shiny we could borrow?"

"Do I ever!" the Wardrobe gushed. Two of her drawers flew open. One contained shiny buttons made of gold, silver, and bronze. The other held crystal beads in all sizes. "Take as many as you need. I've got lots more where these came from!"

"What else do you think we need for our night sky?" Belle asked.

"We need planets!" Chip exclaimed. He raced down the hallway and burst into Cogsworth's quarters. "Cogsworth," he shouted, "can we borrow some gears?"

"Gears?" Cogsworth repeated, confused. His clock hands spun wildly around his face.

"We need them for a very special surprise in the library," Belle explained.

"In that case . . ." Cogsworth began. He opened one of his cupboards and pulled out several gleaming gears. "Will these do?"

"They're perfect!" Chip said.

"Thank you!" Belle called as she followed Chip out of the room.

"Now we need a way to string our stars together," Belle told Chip.

"Maybe Mama has something we can use," Chip said.

As always, Mrs. Potts was delighted to see them. "How about a nice spot of tea?" she asked.

Chip shook his head. "No thanks, Mama. We're working on a big project! Do you have any wire or string?"

"Why, yes, I believe I do," Mrs. Potts said. "This egg basket's not much use to me with that hole. You could unravel it for the wire."

Back in the library, Belle and Chip arranged everything they had gathered on the table. Then they began to build their constellation.

"Chip, we've almost forgotten my favorite thing about constellations," Belle said. "The story!"

"Don't worry," Chip replied. "I know just the story."

Chip told her his idea. "That's perfect!" Belle said.

"But how are we going to hang our constellation in the air?" the little teacup asked.

"I think I know who can help us with that," Belle said. "I'll be right back!"

Belle hurried to the Beast's quarters. When she explained what she and Chip were doing, he happily followed her to the library.

The Beast climbed to the top of a high ladder and hung their constellation. Then he covered it with a large black curtain.

Finally, it was time to invite everyone to see their surprise.

Chip raced around on the tea cart, inviting everyone to the library. When their friends were settled, Belle blew out the candles in the library to make it darker. Then Chip began his story.

"Once upon a time, a girl named Belle got lost in the woods. It was dark and cold outside. And then it began to snow."

Belle scattered paper snowflakes in the air.

"Oooh, lovely, dear," Mrs. Potts said.

"A fine way to set the mood!" Lumiere added.

"Suddenly, a pack of fierce wolves began to chase her!" Chip shouted, making everyone gasp. "The girl was terrified, but she was determined to escape. She ran through the woods, but the wolves followed. They surrounded her. She was sure they were going to devour her. And then, out of nowhere, the Beast showed up and attacked the wolves! He roared and snarled, fighting off the vicious wolves. He tossed one of the wolves so far that it went up, up, up into the sky, where it turned into a constellation for everyone to see. And there it is, to this day, as a reminder not to hurt the Beast's friends!"

As Chip finished his story, Belle pulled down the curtain and unveiled their constellation. Everyone burst into applause!

"Wait, wait, wait," Lumiere said, making his way up to where Belle was standing. "I think you are forgetting one important detail."

Belle and Chip looked at each other, confused. They had stars, planets, and a wonderful story. What had they forgotten?

"The stars are supposed to shine, no?" Lumiere asked with a smile. He pointed his candles up at the constellation, making each bead and button sparkle.

Everyone agreed: now the constellation was perfect!

Disney PRINCESS
Snow White and the Seven Dwarfs

Grumpy's Not Sleepy

D EEP IN THE FOREST, inside a small cottage, Snow White and the Seven Dwarfs were finishing their supper.

"Now, everyone, put your dishes in the tub," Snow White instructed.

Clickety-clack, clickety-clack went the dishes as, one by one, the Dwarfs placed them in the wooden washing tub.

Clickety-clack, clickety-clack, ACHOO!

"Bless you, Sneezy," Snow White said.

"That wasn't me!" Sneezy said.

"Then who was it?" Snow White asked.

"It was—*achoo!*—me—*achoo!*" Grumpy grumbled through a chorus of sneezes.

Snow White put a hand to Grumpy's forehead. "Oh, dear," she said. "You're quite warm! Up to bed with you, right now!"

Snow White and the Dwarfs marched Grumpy upstairs and tucked him into bed.

"Get some sleep, Grumpy," she said. "It will make you feel better."

"This is—*achoo!*—ridiculous!" Grumpy said. "I am not sick. *Achoo! Achoo!* And I have things to do! Do you think that pipe organ is going to—*achoo!*—clean itself?"

"We'll clean it for ya," Happy offered.

The other Dwarfs nodded in agreement.

"You won't do it right," Grumpy said, trying to get out of bed.

"I'm sure they'll do a fine job," Snow White said. "Now, how about a nice song to help you sleep?"

Snow White tucked Grumpy back into bed and began to sing softly
to him. Soon his eyes began to close. He was almost asleep when—

Tooooot! Tooooooot! Tooooooot!

The loud sound came from downstairs.

Grumpy's eyes flew open. "My pipe organ!" he shouted. "I knew
they'd mess it up!"

Snow White hurried downstairs. "You're making too much noise!" she told the Dwarfs.

"But it's a pipe organ," Sleepy pointed out. "We can't clean it without making any . . . *yawn* . . . noise."

"I know!" Doc said. "We can pipe the stuff! I mean stuff the pipes!"

"Now, that's a swell idea!" Happy agreed. "Dopey, grab some socks!"

While Snow White went back up to check on Grumpy, Dopey picked up some socks from the laundry pile. The Dwarfs rolled them into balls and stuffed them into the organ pipes. Then Doc ran a rag over the keys.

Pop! Pop! Pop! The rolled-up socks flew out of the organ pipes.

Bang! Bang! Bang! The socks hit the hanging pots and pans!

Toot! Toot! Toot! the organ sang.

"I heard that!" Grumpy yelled from upstairs. "How do you expect me to sleep with all that racket? *ACHOO!*"

Snow White went back downstairs to see the Dwarfs. "Maybe cleaning the pipe organ can wait until after Grumpy's rested," she said. "Why don't you each pick out a book to read? That's a nice, quiet thing to do."

"Now that's a good my dear—I mean, a good idea!" Doc said.

The Dwarfs hurried to the bookshelf.

"I'd like to read the book about trees," Bashful said shyly.

"I want the story about the treasure—*achoo!*" Sneezy said, standing on his tiptoes to reach over Bashful.

"I'll take the book about birds," Happy said, reaching over Sneezy.

Sleepy reached over Happy. "I'd like that book of . . . *yawn* . . . bedtime stories."

Doc reached over Sleepy. "Dopey and I will read the—"

Doc tripped and fell onto Sleepy, who crashed into Happy, who knocked over Sneezy and Bashful, who fell into the bookshelf. The books fell to the floor with a crash!

"I *heard* that!" Grumpy yelled downstairs.

"Oh, dear," Snow White said. "Perhaps you should go outside so poor Grumpy can get some sleep."

Snow White shooed the Dwarfs into the yard, then went upstairs to check on Grumpy.

"What do we do now?" Happy asked.

"Maybe we could find a way to help Snow White," Bashful suggested shyly.

"A fine idea!" Doc said, looking around. "Hmmm . . . these windows look like they could use some washing."

The Dwarfs got to work. Dopey fetched water from the stream. Happy and Sleepy got the ladder. Bashful got some rags. Then Sneezy climbed the ladder, holding the bucket and the rags.

"All right there, Sneezy!" Doc called up. "Start scrubbing!"

"Doc," Bashful said quietly, "are you sure it's a good idea to send Sneezy up there?"

"He'll be fine," Doc said. "What could go wrong?"

"ACHOO!"

Sneezy let out a great big sneeze and fell off the ladder, right into Happy's and Sleepy's waiting arms.

The ladder crashed into the laundry line, and the clean laundry fell into the mud! The water bucket landed on a basket of potatoes, which spilled on the ground. As the Dwarfs tried to get out of the way, they tripped over the potatoes.

"I *heard* that!" Grumpy yelled from his bed.

Snow White came outside. "I suppose it's no use asking you to be quiet anymore," she said. "But please, clean up this mess!"

The Dwarfs nodded. While Snow White went in to take care of Grumpy, they got to work. They rewashed all the laundry and hung it out to dry. They picked up the potatoes. They fixed the ladder and the bucket.

Soon they were all yawning.

"All this work is making me sleepy," Sleepy said.

"Me too," agreed Doc, Bashful, Happy, and Sneezy. Dopey nodded.

"I think you could all use a nice nap," Snow White said walking outside again. The Dwarfs didn't argue. They marched upstairs, and Snow White tucked them into their beds.

Soon they were all snoring peacefully—even Grumpy!

Disney
PRINCESS

Cinderella
Bedtime for Gus

CINDERELLA LOOKED OUT HER window. The sun was setting. In the distance, she could see the castle's clock. It read eight o'clock.

Cinderella tapped gently on the walls of her attic room. "Bedtime!" she called.

Jaq, Suzy, Gus, and the other mice hurried out of their mouse hole. Cinderella did all the household chores in her wicked stepmother's house. She never had time for fun, so the birds and mice were her only friends.

"Bedtime already?" Jaq cried.

"Buh-bedtime?" Gus asked.

Gus was Cinderella's newest mouse friend. She had just rescued him from a trap that morning.

"Bedtime, Gus-Gus. Close eyes and . . . *zzzz* . . . fall asleep!" Suzy explained.

Gus looked confused. He closed his eyes and started to tip over.

Jaq caught him. "Not *fall*, Gus-Gus," he said. "Fall asleep. Like this."
He put his head on his hands and pretended to snore.

Cinderella laughed. "Falling asleep isn't all there is to bedtime," she
said. "Gus has never lived in a house before. We'll have to teach him
about getting ready for bed."

"Okay! Okay!" the other mice cried. "Show Gus-Gus!"

"First," Cinderella said, "you have to put on your pajamas." She went to a trunk and pulled out a tiny pair of striped pajamas for Gus. "Here, try these on."

Soon they were all in their pajamas—even Cinderella.

"That's better," Cinderella declared. "Pajamas are much more comfortable for sleeping than regular clothes."

Gus nodded. "Gus-Gus loves pajamas!" he exclaimed. "Gus-Gus wear pajamas all the time!"

Cinderella smiled. "I'm glad you like your pajamas, Gus, but they are only for while you're sleeping."

The mouse nodded.

"Now sleep, Cinderella?" another mouse cried.

Cinderella smiled. "Not quite yet," she said to the young mouse. "First, wash your face and bush your teeth. When you're all scrubbed and brushed, I'll kiss you good night, and then Suzy will tuck everyone in."

The mice began to brush their teeth.

"Mmm-mmm," Gus said with a smile, tasting the minty toothpaste.

The other mice giggled and finished up. Gus watched carefully. Before long, he was done, too.

"Tuh-tuck in?" Gus asked.

Jaq pulled him toward the washbasin. "Not yet, Gus-Gus," he said. He handed him some soap.

Gus looked puzzled. But he watched as the other mice washed their faces and patted themselves dry with old rags. Then he did the same thing.

When the mice were all neat and clean, Cinderella kissed them good night. "It's time for everyone to go to sleep," she said sweetly.

"Follow me," Jaq told Gus. He ran to his little bed and hopped in. Then he pointed to the bed next to him. "That's your bed," he said.

Gus grinned and got under the covers.

Suzy tucked in each of the mice.

"Story, Cinderelly!" the mice cried. "Story!"

Cinderella smiled. "All right," she said. "Once upon a time, there was a young prince who lived in a beautiful castle. He had everything that money could buy—fine clothes, jewels, paintings, and more. But something was missing. He didn't have anyone special to love. . . ."

Cinderella continued the story for a long time. Each time she tried to stop, the mice begged for more. After a while, they couldn't keep their eyes open anymore. It was just too late.

When the last mouse had fallen asleep, Cinderella tiptoed to her own bed and climbed in, still thinking about her bedtime story. Dreaming up tales made her forget her life of chores, at least for a time.

Just then, Gus began to snore. Cinderella giggled and pulled up her covers. She glanced once more at the clock on the castle tower. It read eleven o'clock. "Oh, my," she murmured sleepily. "If the mice had their way, I'd be telling tales until midnight!"

Cinderella snuggled against her pillow and yawned. "If only some of my stories would come true . . ." she added sleepily.

As Cinderella closed her eyes, the birds began to sing a lullaby. Soon Cinderella was fast asleep, dreaming that someday she'd meet a handsome prince and live happily ever after.

BRAVE

The Princess
and the Kelpie

MERIDA WAS FRUSTRATED. HER mum's birthday was coming up, and she was trying to draw a picture for her. But no matter what she drew, nothing felt quite right.

"Why can't I figure out what to draw?" Merida asked Maudie. "It shouldn't be that hard!"

"Cheer up, lassie," Maudie replied. "It will come to you when the time is right."

Merida set down her quill. She was about to fetch a snack when she heard commotion outside the door. Peering into the hallway, she spotted her brothers—Hubert, Hamish, and Harris—chasing each other.

"Och! It's past your bedtime," she said. "What are you wee devils still doing up and about?"

"We can't sleep," Hubert answered.

"We need a bedtime story," Hamish explained.

"A scary one!" Harris added.

Merida marched into the hall and scooped up her brothers.

"Come on," she said sternly. "Off to bed with the lot of you."

The triplets squirmed, but Merida was stronger than they were, and in no time she had all three of them tucked into bed.

"Now, let's see," Merida said, looking at the boys' books. "A scary story. Och. This one will do nicely!"

Merida pulled a book from the shelf and sat down to read to the triplets. "Here we go," she began. *"The Princess and the Kelpie."*

"A princess story?" Hubert asked. "What's scary about that?"

"Now, now," Merida said. "No back talk. You asked for a scary story, and that's what you'll get."

"What's a kelpie?" Hamish asked.

Merida smiled. "You'll see soon enough," she answered.

Merida opened the book and began.

"Once upon a time, there was a brave princess. One day, the princess decided to go out for a ride on her noble steed. As they approached the woods, the princess saw a gray flash pass before her eyes. Her horse bucked, but the princess was not afraid. 'Don't be a ninny,' she told her horse. 'Come on, now. Let's see what it was!'

"The two had not gone far when they came upon a gray horse. Its coat shimmered and its mane looked like fine silk. The princess had never seen such an animal. She stepped forward, careful not to spook the stallion. But her own horse stood in her way.

"'Now, now,' the princess said. 'This horse may be lost. It may need our help.'

"The princess's horse gave a soft whine and then stepped aside. With a stomp of its hoof, the stallion lowered its head. The princess reached out and touched its silky mane.

"'Well, now, aren't you a bonnie lad,' she said. Then, grabbing hold of the horse's mane, she swung up onto its back.

"The horse reared up. It tried to buck, but the princess stayed on. She had been riding horses her whole life and knew she could control this one, even without a bridle.

"Suddenly, the horse charged forward. The princess tried to calm him, but it was no use. The mighty stallion refused to slow down. And worse, he was headed straight for a deep loch!

"The princess tried to free her hands of the horse's mane, but they were stuck. Her legs were stuck, too!

"The princess knew there was only one thing that could cause this. There must be some auld faerie magic at work.

"The princess tried to pull her hands free again. If she didn't find a way to stop the stallion, he was going to run both of them over a cliff and straight into the deep water!

"Just then, the horse brushed against a tree. Some of the morning dew fell from a branch and landed on one of the princess's hands. At once, her hand slid free of the stallion's mane.

"Now the princess understood. She had come upon not simply a lost horse, but rather upon a kelpie—a mysterious water spirit. The princess shivered. She was in more danger than she'd thought. The kelpie was not a kind creature. It delighted in casting unsuspecting riders into the sea.

"The princess looked ahead of her. The kelpie was drawing closer and closer to the edge of the cliff!

"But the princess was wise, and she knew that there was one way to stop a kelpie. She needed a bridle. Only then would the horse do her bidding.

"With a loud whistle, the princess called for her horse. The noble creature charged forward to catch up with the princess. Then, using the hand that had come free, the princess wrestled the bridle off her own horse and onto the kelpie. With the reins in her hand, she guided the horse to a path that led away from the cliff.

"As they reached the shore of the loch, the kelpie came to a stop. As if by magic, the princess's hand and legs were freed. She slipped off the mysterious horse.

"The stallion stood quietly, looking at the princess. She gazed deeply into the kelpie's eyes. Then, with a nod, she removed the bridle.

"The kelpie shook its head and turned toward the water. The princess watched in amazement as it stepped into the loch and slowly disappeared. Then, climbing atop her own horse, the princess returned home."

Merida closed the book. "Well, lads. What did you think? A fine story, was it not?"

But Merida's brothers did not answer. They had fallen fast asleep.

Merida shrugged. "*I* thought it was scary," she said.

Setting the book down, she quietly tiptoed out of the boys' room.

Merida walked down the hall to her own room. Maudie had been right. While she had been reading to the triplets, an idea had come to her for her drawing.

Merida lit a candle. Then she took out a fresh piece of parchment and got to work. She was sure her mum would love the drawing!

Disney
Aladdin
Abu Monkeys Around

ONE SUNNY MORNING, ABU the monkey swung through the marketplace of Agrabah. His friends Aladdin, the Genie, Jasmine, and Rajah strolled slowly along the street below him.

All was calm and quiet—too quiet! Abu, who loved nothing more than making mischief, looked around. His gaze landed on a stand overflowing with ripe bananas. That gave him an idea.

The little monkey swung over to the stand and snatched up a banana. He tore it open, shoved the fruit into his mouth, and then dropped the peel on the ground.

Abu grabbed another banana and did the same thing. And then another, and another! Soon the street was covered in banana peels. Then Abu started jumping up and down and screeching loudly. Waving his hands in the air, he tried to get his friends' attention.

Aladdin, Jasmine, Rajah, and the Genie hurried over to the little monkey. They were so focused on reaching Abu that they didn't see the banana peels. They slipped and slid until they landed in a heap on the ground!

Abu chattered happily to himself and laughed at his friends. They had looked so silly tripping over the banana peels! But his friends were not laughing with him.

"Bad Abu!" Aladdin said, helping Jasmine up. "We could have really gotten hurt!"

Abu hung his head and followed his friends back to the palace. He watched as they carefully laid out the food they'd bought at the market.

Soon everyone was enjoying a nice snack in the courtyard— everyone but Abu.

The little monkey eyed the fountain. The water looked nice and cool. And it *was* awfully hot out.

Abu grinned. He had another idea.

Abu waited until everyone was done eating. He watched as his friends
sat down at the edge of the fountain for a rest.

Then . . . *SPLASH!*

Abu did a big cannonball right into the water!

Abu's friends jumped up, drenched by the cold water. The Genie was so startled that he fell backward, right into the fountain! Rajah growled at the little monkey. The tiger did *not* like being wet.

Abu giggled. He was pleased with his mischief. But his friends did not find it as funny.

"Bad Abu," Jasmine said. "It's not nice to splash."

Wringing out her hair, Jasmine went inside to dry off. The rest of her friends followed.

That night, as the moon rose high over Agrabah, Abu crept through the palace.

He was walking past Jasmine's room when he heard a loud noise. It was Rajah. The tiger was snoring!

Abu grinned. With everyone asleep, the palace was far too quiet. Luckily, he knew just how to fix that!

Abu scurried to his collection of treasures and grabbed a wooden mallet. He dragged it into the hallway and hit it against every door he passed. Finally, Abu reached the throne room. The Genie's lamp was resting on a pillow.

Abu lifted the wooden mallet over the lamp and . . .

BANG!

Abu hit the mallet against the lamp. The Genie rose out of his lamp in a plume of curling blue smoke.

"Wha—I'm here! My wish is your command! I mean, your wish . . ."

Genie shook his head, confused. Then he noticed Abu laughing. "Bad Abu," he said. "Don't you know that genies need their beauty sleep?"

Just then, a very groggy Rajah came into the room. He was followed by a yawning Aladdin and a sleepy-looking Jasmine.

"Abu . . . buddy. You've been monkeying around *all* day," Aladdin said. "Aren't you *tired*?"

"It's bedtime, Abu," Jasmine said sweetly.

Rajah nodded and groaned.

"Come on, pal. How about some rest?" the Genie said.

But Abu didn't answer.

"Abu?" Aladdin asked, looking for his friend.

"Ummm . . . Aladdin," Jasmine said, pointing across the room.

Aladdin followed her gaze. Abu had curled up on the Genie's pillow and fallen fast asleep.

The Genie grabbed a blanket and laid it over the monkey. "Good Abu," he said.

And with that, the friends crept out of the room to let Abu get some sleep.